This book should be returned to any branch of the
Lancashire County Library on or before the date shown

'The Freezosaurus'
An original concept by Jenny Jinks
© Jenny Jinks

Illustrated by Daniel Limon (Beehive Illustration)

Published by MAVERICK ARTS PUBLISHING LTD
Studio 3A, City Business Centre, 6 Brighton Road,
Horsham, West Sussex, RH13 5BB
© Maverick Arts Publishing Limited November 2018
+44 (0)1403 256941

A CIP catalogue record for this book is available at the British Library.

ISBN 978-1-84886-389-7

www.maverickbooks.co.uk

Gold

This book is rated as: Gold Band (Guided Reading)

The
FREEZOSAURUS

By Jenny Jinks   Illustrated by Daniel Limon

Chapter 1

Freddie was mad about dinosaurs. He had dinosaur pyjamas, dinosaur wallpaper, and a dinosaur lunch bag. Freddie even cut his food into dinosaur shapes.

Freddie's class were going on a trip to the museum. They had a huge dinosaur exhibit there. Freddie couldn't wait.

"Wow!" Freddie said when they got inside.

There was a giant skeleton as tall as the roof. Freddie didn't know what to look at first.

As Freddie looked around, his bag knocked an egg off the display.

The egg landed with a crash and rolled away. Freddie chased after it. When he picked it up, the egg had a huge crack in it.

"Oh no!" said Freddie. He looked around,

but everyone had gone.

Freddie put the egg in his lunch bag. He would tell someone about it later, he thought. Then he ran to catch up with his class.

But in all the excitement, Freddie forgot about the egg.

On the bus on the way home, Freddie heard TAP! TAP! TAP! It was coming from his lunch bag.

Freddie unzipped it and looked inside. There was the dinosaur egg.

TAP! TAP! TAP!

As Freddie watched, the egg cracked more and more. Little bits of shell started breaking off. Something was alive inside.

The egg was hatching!

Chapter 2

Finally a big piece of shell broke off.

Freddie could see a tiny dinosaur inside.
It had a big head, a long tail, and little wings
on its back. Its blue shiny skin sparkled in
the light.

It didn't look like any of the dinosaurs
Freddie had seen in his books.

The tiny dinosaur let out a sneeze.

ACHOOOOO!

The water in Freddie's water bottle froze.

"Shhhh!" Freddie whispered, shutting his bag quickly. He didn't want anyone to see. The dinosaur would be his secret.

When Freddie got home, he quickly took the dinosaur up to his room.

"I wish I knew what type of dinosaur you are," said Freddie.

The little dinosaur gave another sneeze. Tiny icicles shot out of his nose.

He sneezed again and the water on Freddie's bedside table turned to ice.

"You're a Freezosaurus!" laughed Freddie. "But I'll call you Frozo."

Freddie kept Frozo hidden in his room. He played with him all afternoon.

Frozo tried flapping his little wings, and soon he was flying around Freddie's room, freezing everything in sight.

When his mum came to say goodnight, Freddie hid Frozo under his covers.

"You can share my bed with me," Freddie said kindly.

But Frozo didn't look very happy. He wasn't feeling well. He was getting very hot.

Freddie had to do something. And fast!

Then Freddie had an idea.

"I bet you need to be kept cold," he said.

Freddie tucked Frozo inside his pyjama pocket and crept downstairs. Frozo sneezed again.

"Shhhh!" Freddie whispered. He didn't want his mum to hear.

He went into the kitchen and put Frozo in the freezer. He tucked him under a blanket of frozen peas. Frozo looked better already.

"You stay there," Freddie said. "And try to be quiet!"

Frozo smiled and snuggled down for the night.

Chapter 3

The next day Freddie took Frozo to school. He kept him in his lunch bag to keep him cool.

All of Freddie's friends loved Frozo. They couldn't believe that Freddie had a real dinosaur as a pet.

When Freddie took Frozo out at lunch time, Frozo turned everyone's drinks into ice lollies. Then he turned the playground into an ice rink. The children had the best time skating around. Having Frozo at school was so much fun.

Just then Frozo flew up into the clouds.

"Come back!" Freddie cried.

Suddenly it started to snow.

The children spent the afternoon building snowmen and having snowball fights. The teachers couldn't understand why it was snowing in the summer. They had no idea about Frozo, hidden in Freddie's pocket.

Freddie took Frozo everywhere with him. Frozo's favourite place was the supermarket. He loved playing in the huge freezers, eating all the ice.

But Frozo was getting bigger and bigger, and harder to hide.

One day Freddie heard a scream from the kitchen. He rushed to see what was wrong.

"What is this?" Mum said. "And why is it in my freezer?"

She had found Frozo.

"Don't worry," said Freddie. "He won't hurt you."

Freddie picked Frozo up. He explained what had happened at the museum, and how he had accidentally brought Frozo home.

"You can't keep a dinosaur as a pet," said Mum. "We have to take him back."

Chapter 4

Mum rang the museum. Some men in white coats came round to see Frozo. They wanted to take him away and do lots of tests.

Frozo did not like the men. He didn't want any scary tests. He hid behind Freddie.

"Please don't make him go with them," Freddie begged his mum.

"I'm sorry, there's been a mistake," Mum told the men. "Frozo is staying with us."

"Thank you!" Freddie said, hugging his mum.

But Frozo kept getting bigger. He no longer

fitted in the freezer. And he kept freezing things by mistake.

"I'm sorry," said Mum. "But we can't keep Frozo anymore. It's not fair to him."

Mum rang lots of places to find a home for

Frozo. But nobody had room for a huge ice breathing dinosaur.

Finally a nature centre up in the mountains agreed to take him. It sounded perfect. The centre was big, and it was cold – just what Frozo needed.

Even so, Freddie didn't want him to go.

When the man came to collect Frozo, Freddie couldn't bear to say goodbye.

"I'll miss you," Freddie said. Frozo lifted Freddie up for one last hug.

Chapter 5

Life wasn't the same without Frozo. School wasn't as much fun anymore, Freddie's drinks were always warm, there were no more snowball fights, and even trips to the shops were boring.

Freddie missed Frozo. So did all of his friends.

"Cheer up," said Mum. "We're going to visit

Frozo next week."

Freddie couldn't wait. He counted down the days until he would see his best friend again.

When Freddie got to the nature centre it was better than he'd imagined. It was a huge winter wonderland. Everywhere was covered in ice and snow. But how was he ever going to find Frozo?

Then a huge snowball came rolling down the hill towards Freddie. But it wasn't a snowball at all. It was Frozo!

He barrelled into Freddie, knocking him over. Freddie jumped on top of Frozo and gave him a huge hug.

"I've missed you, Frozo," said Freddie.

Freddie spent ages playing with Frozo.
It was just like old times.

Freddie could see how happy Frozo was in his new home. Even though Freddie missed Frozo more than anything, Freddie knew he was in the right place now. When it was time for Freddie to go he didn't want to leave.

Freddie visited Frozo as often as he could. Frozo became famous all around the world. People came from miles around to visit the giant ice-breathing dinosaur. Everybody loved him.

But no one loved him more than Freddie.

The End

Book Bands for Guided Reading

The Institute of Education book banding system is a scale of colours that reflects the various levels of reading difficulty. The bands are assigned by taking into account the content, the language style, the layout, phonics and a range of other word level work.

Maverick Early Readers are a bright, attractive range of books covering the pink to white bands. All of these books have been book banded for guided reading to the industry standard and edited by a leading educational consultant.

To view the whole Maverick Readers scheme, visit our website at

www.maverickearlyreaders.com

Or scan the QR code above to view our scheme instantly!

Pink

Red

Yellow

Blue

Green

Orange

Turquoise

Purple

Gold

White